PROPERTY OF
INDEPENDENT SCHOOL DIST. No. 1

# ZOO, WHERE ARE YOU?

by Ann McGovern

*Illustrated by Ezra Jack Keats*

Josh had no zoo in his town or even nearby, so he decided to catch his own animals for his own zoo. He set out with animal-hunting equipment — whistles and ropes and things — singing, not too loud to frighten the animals, "Zoo, zoo, where are you?" There might be a giraffe or a zebra, but all he found was an acorn, a rusty key, a wooden wheel, a red leaf and other assorted junk. It was beautiful junk when he got it all together, and he didn't have to bother with cages or feed — he could enjoy just looking. He had his very own zoo.

Classification and Dewey Decimal: Easy (E)

## *About the Author:*

ANN McGOVERN enjoys writing historical and biographical as well as imaginative stories for young children. Born in Brooklyn, New York, she studied at the University of New Mexico and has traveled extensively. She has written book reviews and has been an editor for a New York publishing firm. She now lives in Paris, France.

## *About the Illustrator:*

Although he has been a muralist and exhibited in various galleries, EZRA JACK KEATS loves writing and illustrating children's books more than working in any other field. A Caldecott Medal winner, Mr. Keats has lived and painted in Paris.

For the pond and the woods—and the Langners—at Still Hill Road.
And for Peter who visits.

DISCARD

10¢

# ZOO, WHERE

Text copyright © 1964 by Ann McGovern   Pictures copyright © 1964 by Ezra Jack Keats
Printed in the United States of America. All rights reserved. Library of Congress Catalog Card Number : 64-16659
This edition lithographed in U.S.A. by Wetzel Brothers, Inc., Milwaukee, Wisconsin

# ARE YOU?

by Ann McGovern

## Pictures by Ezra Jack Keats

1968 FIRST CADMUS EDITION
THIS SPECIAL EDITION IS PUBLISHED BY ARRANGEMENT WITH
THE PUBLISHERS OF THE REGULAR EDITION
HARPER & ROW, PUBLISHERS, INCORPORATED
BY
**E. M. HALE AND COMPANY**
EAU CLAIRE, WISCONSIN

There was no zoo in Josh's town.
Not outside the town.
Not inside the town.
No zoo for miles around.

Josh wanted a zoo with lions roaring, tigers
growling, monkeys grinning, snakes slithering.
But there was no zoo.

"There's nothing else to do," said Josh one day,
"except to make a zoo myself.
"I'll go to the pond. I'll go to the woods.
"And I'll come home with a zoo of my own.
"Let's see," said Josh, looking around.
"I'll need some things:

> a wild-animal-catching bag,
> a hunter's gun,
> a glass jar,
> heavy ropes,
> and a whistle for calling animals."

He told his mother he was going to collect a zoo.
She gave him an apple and some cookies
and kissed him good-bye.
Josh's cat wanted to come along, but Josh said,
"No. Stay here. It might be dangerous."

PROPERTY OF
INDEPENDENT SCHOOL DIST. No. 4

He felt bold and fearless as he walked
down the road
to the pond.
"Zoo, zoo, where are you, zoo?" he sang.
He didn't sing it too loud. He didn't want
to frighten away his zoo.

There might be a snapping-jawed alligator
swimming under the water.
Or a fat baby hippo taking a mud bath.

But all he saw at the pond was the sun shining
on the water and the trees looking twice their size.
Josh sat at the edge of the pond.
No alligator.
No hippo.
But there—lying on the ground,
sparkling in the sun,
was a smooth piece of green glass.
Josh picked it up and put it into his
wild-animal-catching bag.

Then he began to look for his zoo again.
He found a wooden wheel
that nobody wanted anymore.
Then he found a red leaf.
He put them in his bag.
Just then the grass moved near his feet.

A frog hopped past, fast.
Quickly Josh grabbed for the frog,
but it was gone.
He found a ball where the frog had been.
So he put the ball in his bag.

He looked in the weeds for a wild goose.
He didn't find a wild goose,
but he found an acorn with its cap on.
He looked in the mud for a mud turtle.
He didn't find a mud turtle,
but he found an old picture.
He walked all around the pond, looking for zoo animals.
He found a rusty key and a branch shaped like an arrow.

Then he was hungry, so he went home for lunch.
"Well," said his mother, "what did you find?"
"Junk," said Josh, emptying his bag on the kitchen table
for his mother to see. "Isn't it beautiful?"
"Beautiful," said his mother.
And it was.

PROPERTY OF
INDEPENDENT SCHOOL DIST. No. 4

After lunch Josh went out again. He felt bold and fearless
as he walked down the road to the woods.
"Zoo, zoo, where are you, zoo?" he sang.
He didn't sing it too loud.
He didn't want to frighten away his zoo.
There might be a giraffe chewing on the top of a tree.
Or a striped zebra.

But all he saw in the woods was the sun shining
through the tall trees in patches. And some violets growing
close to the earth. Josh sat down on the cool ground.
No giraffe.
No zebra.
But there—right next to him was a bent stick.
Josh picked it up and put it into his bag.

Josh looked behind a tree for a lion.
He didn't find a lion, but he found a long chain.
He looked in the bushes for a wolf.
He didn't find a wolf, but he found a pair of eyeglasses
without any glass.
"The animals will come if I call them with my whistle,"
thought Josh. He blew a loud blast.

Stirring of leaves. Whirring of wings.
Silence, then, and sun and shade.
Suddenly Josh's heart pounded.
What was that, crashing through the bushes?
*A bear?*
Josh wanted a bear for his zoo. But not now!
The crashing sound came closer and closer.
Josh ran and ran until he didn't hear it anymore.

"That was a narrow escape," he said, leaning against a tree.
Then he found a brass knob and a feather.
"It's time to go home," Josh thought. "Anyway, that bear
might have a brother bear someplace around here."
So Josh slung his bag over his shoulder and walked home.

PROPERTY OF
INDEPENDENT SCHOOL DIST. No. 4

"Well," said his mother, "what did you find this time?"

"More junk," said Josh. "Isn't it beautiful?"

"More beautiful," said his mother.

And it was.

After supper Josh said, "I've tried collecting
my zoo in the morning.

"I've tried collecting my zoo in the afternoon.

"Maybe I'll have more luck at night."

He felt bold and fearless as he walked out the back
door to the backyard.

He took his cat with him for protection.

"Zoo, zoo, where are you, zoo?" he sang.
He didn't sing it too loud.
He didn't want to frighten away his zoo.

There might be an owl with shiny yellow eyes.
Or a panther behind a shadow.

But all he saw was a dark night carpet
spread way over his head. And a sliver of moon.
Josh sat down on the back steps.
No owl.
No panther.
But there—flying near—were pinpoints of light.
*Fireflies!*
Josh caught a few and put them into his jar.
He ran inside to show them to his mother.
But as soon as he was inside the house,
the fireflies changed into plain flies.
Josh ran outside and set them free.
And they were fireflies again.

Then he found a white rock
and an old dump truck he had lost long ago.
He looked at his hunter's gun.
And his heavy ropes.
And the whistle for calling animals.
All these he put into his bag.
His mother called, "Time to go to bed, Josh."
So he went inside.

"Well," said his mother, "what did you find this time?"

"Even more junk," said Josh.

"Isn't it beautiful?"

"Even more beautiful," said his mother.

And it was.

"Even more beautiful than a zoo," said Josh.

Then he made a discovery.

"But this *is* a zoo," he said. "It's a zooful of junk.

"And I don't have to put my zoo in cages or feed it

or try to make it happy.

"I can just look at it and look at it and look at it."

Josh took his zooful of beautiful junk to bed with him. Before he
fell asleep, he made up a song which he sang over and over:
>
> Oh, zoo, zoo, zoo,
> I love you so,
> From my head to my toe,
> I do, I do, I do,
> I love you, zoo.